T.M. Cooks is the pen name of the following collaborative writing team. The contributors are:

- Amber Preece

- Archie Jordan

- Owen Morris

- Claudia Delicata

- Dilara Hayward

- Emily Smith

- Freya Wilson

- Grace Gething-Murfin

- Marc Brizan

- Max Bailey

- Abigail Pye

- Holly Smith

with cover design by Morgan. The project was overseen by Joe Reddington, Dr Yvonne Skipper and Richard Seymour.

The group cheerfully acknowledges the wonderful help given by:

- Emily Stanway

- Louise Beardmore

And a big thank you goes to Higher Horizons who funded this wonderful project. Its been a wonderful opportunity, and everyone involved has been filled with incredible knowledge and enthusiasm.

Finally, we would like to thank all staff at Trentham Academy for their support in releasing our novelists from lessons for a full week.

The group started to plan out their novel at 9.00 on Monday 9th May 2022 and completed their last proof reading at 14.40 on Friday 13th May 2022.

We are incredibly proud to state that every word of the story, every idea, every chapter and yes, every mistake, is entirely their own work. No teachers, parents or other students touched a single key during this process, and we would ask readers to keep this in mind.

We are sure you will agree that this is an incredible achievement. It has been a true delight and privilege to see this group of young people turn into professional novelists in front of our very eyes.

The Deviants

T. M. Cooks

0

Contents

Chapter 1

Ramesses II

Smoke billowed from uncontrollable fires that lit up the soul-sucking gloom. Clouds of smog hung low, consuming the inhabitants' lungs. The constant crunch as the demons of hell stumbled across the bone covered floor echoed throughout the abyss. Screams could be heard as fires burnt the skin of the beings who crossed them. The blood splatters decorated the fiery pit. Hell treated everyone as equally awful as everyone else, no matter who you were or where you came from.

Ramesses II, an Egyptian pharaoh, was lost in the depths of hell. Irritated and flustered he dived to the side, narrowly avoiding a large flying object that looked suspiciously like a decapitated head. In his eyes he was a God, however unfortunately for him, most other people disagreed with him. Most saw him as a master, an evil and very self-centred being. Ramesses would complain to anyone about how he doesn't belong in 'this pit of doom.' Anyone that he said that to would laugh at him, thinking that he was joking, before walking away as quickly as they could without running when they realised that he was being serious. People thought that he was delusional.

Ramesses would often tell people that he would do anything to get out of the 'pit of doom' that he was trapped in. Everyone would laugh at him and tell him that there is no possible way to escape, but little did everyone know that he had feared that what was happening would happen and had planned an escape route before he died. He just needed a very specific person to come to his rescue...

8

Chapter 2

Backstabber

Elijah walked in from work, slamming the front door. Loosening his tie, Kate walked through the foyer - plodding on the wooden floor. She pointed her finger at him, her face scrunching up with every word she forced through gritted teeth. He peered over at George, who was sat on the sofa with his headphones, playing his video games. He looked so oblivious to what was happening.

"You're always back late! I'm always juggling everything on my own! George, cooking, cleaning!" Kate screamed. Elijah looked down at the floor, sighing heavily and barged past her in frustration.

"Don't you barge past me! I'm trying to talk to you! You never listen - just forget it; like you normally do." She muttered the last bit to herself and Elijah shook his head irritatedly.

Kate walked back to the kitchen, returning to her ironing. The once massive pile was now three quarters of the way finished, and she was still muttering to herself.

"I really can't be arsed with this today, " Elijah huffed through his clenched jaw, slipping his shoes off in the process.

When all of a sudden, something switched in Elijah's head. Something strange. Something manipulative. Something violent.

Elijah walked silently through the hallway, the

lights standing upright on the flowery green wall-paper. Kate was stood with her back to the kitchen door. He opened the dark oak drawers, grabbing the large kitchen knife slowly. It made a scraping sound against the oak, dragging it away from its once safe place. He stepped closer and closer towards her. Towards the once love of his life.

Before she could bend over, the knife exerted itself against the small of her back, he grabbed the iron and shoved it into her porcelain skin. Screams filled the room, bouncing from wall to wall. Screams of agony. Screams of fear. Elijah pushed the iron further into her, disfiguring her once beautiful face. Elijah held her up as his knife stabbed her.

And again. And again.

Kate went limp. She was now just a lifeless body.

Elijah shakily picked the iron up from her face, sizzling as it arose. He placed the iron onto the ironing board, a salty barbecued aroma filled his nostrils.

11

"When did I last eat?" He thought to himself as he began trembling. His hands were tremoring uncontrollably - the knife dropping as a repercussion of his unwanted shaking limbs.

"Why am I shaking?" He questioned to himself "Stop it!"

He stood up abruptly - the knife clashing down onto the floor. Blood pooling out of her back, surrounding her. It was matted with her charred hair like a wildfire had torn through her scalp relentlessly.

Tears threatened to fall from his eyes as his once beautiful wife lay there.

Dead.

One managed to escape, dropping onto her fourth degree burn. Searing as it slid down her face. He wiped his face quickly, brushing away the grief that burdened his soul.

Kate's limp body was lifted from the ground, her head and legs swinging as Elijah carried her away from her metaphorical death bed. He walked out of the back door, feeling it would be smart to keep a dead body out of George's view. He opened the car boot with one of his hands, struggling slightly before he shoved her inside.

Taking one last look at Kate, he slammed the boot shut - shadows covering her body. Still shaking, Elijah walked over to the driver side of the car, looking over at the large window that uncovered the living room area - and there sat George. Unaware. Unaware that his mother was laying lifeless in the boot of his family car. Unaware that there is mass amounts of blood laying on the kitchen floor. Hopefully he wouldn't go in. Hopefully he would continue playing his game. It's not like Elijah is going to be long, just a quick nip out.

He half-heartedly smiles as he watched his son, before he clambered into the car. The ignition turned, churning as he turned the key. The radio began blaring music, and Elijah slammed the knob, turning it off instantly. He couldn't deal with the loud sounds right now - the mourning was too strong for him to cope. Looking behind him, he reversed out of the drive, sighing and putting

13

it into drive, accelerating off.

Elijah sped down the road, doing at least sixty miles per hour on a forty miles per hour road. Trees and bushes were blurring into a green mess. The odd occasional yellow and fuchsia flowers creating a spark of brightness, but it was mainly just a blur of green nothingness.

Dusk had finally began to creep in, casting ominous shadows on the road. Trees began to wave in the wind, and rain began pouring out of the drab clouds. The winder wipers dragged across the window, picking up the pace as the rain continued heavier. A deep rumble echoed through the trees. Shaking the trunks of the trees violently. Elijah's knuckles turned an off-white colour as he gripped tighter and tighter on the steering wheel.

A scream ripped through his mouth, trapped in the confinement of the car. He banged on the steering wheel, tears now gushing out of his eyes. He pulled over to a lay-by, hitting his steering wheel continuously. His screams got louder, and his wails became more prominent. Bouncing to-and-fro from each window. Screams of sadness. Screams of anguish. Screams of regret. Trying to calm himself down, he rolled down his window, squinting his eyes as the rain and his tears worked as a disadvantage for his vision.

A lake.

It was sitting there, lonely. Nobody around for miles. He quickly got out of the car, promptly moving towards the boot. Opening it up, he grabbed Kate's body. Picking up the weight of his grief. The weight of all the memories they used to share, now they're gone. Just like her. He slung her over his shoulders, closing the boot harshly. Marching through the marshy green.

Trekking through the swamp-like grass was hard enough. But the weight of the body and guilt on his shoulders was most definitely worse. He reached the lake, which was creating an optical il-lusion as rain droplets fell gracefully onto the lake. His toes were on the edge of the lake, his pointy shoes balancing precariously on the edge.

Pulling her off his shoulders, he was now holding her bridal style. Yet, Kate wasn't laughing like she normally was - her eyes were open but there was no light behind them. No chandelier-like glimmer. Just an empty void. With one hand supporting her back, he lifted the other up to the back of her head, running his fingers through her matted hair. The once perfect eyeliner was now smudged from tears, and he hesitantly wiped it clean. A single tear drop fell from his lubricated eye, onto her forehead. He craned his neck towards her face and kissed her pale forehead - wiping the salty tear away.

Elijah smiled timidly, dropping her body into the lake. It splashed loudly, and the once murky water became a deep maroon colour as her blood merged with the contaminated water and her body sunk deeper and deeper into the lake.

Without looking back, he walked back to his stranded car. The hazard lights were on and the driver side door was still open, until Elijah climbed inside and slammed it shut. Leaning over, he opened the glovebox and inside a brown, leather bound book lay there direly. He looked at it tentatively before looking back at the road.

A sense of certainty filled his lungs. He smiled almost knowingly and put the car back into second gear. Pulling off from the lay-by, he closed the glovebox whilst pressing the volume knob to the radio, turning it up loudly. Speeding away from the murder he had just committed, humming nonchalantly to a familiar tune on the radio and tapping his hand on the steering wheel.

The radio presenter began talking as the song finished, making an unfunny joke. Elijah smiled and hummed in laughter.

Suddenly, a song came on the radio. It was Kate and Elijah's wedding song. His smile faded, and the sound of his tapping slowly stopped. Tears began streaming from his eyes once again, dropping onto his hands and falling onto his silver wedding ring.

He looks over at the side of the road, it was steep. Very steep. If a car went crashing over that cliff then surely he would die. It would end all of his suffering. His cries grew louder and he shouted for his wife.

"KATE!" He shouts. "Oh Kate!" He pauses, sniffling as if expecting an answer. "Come back to me, Kate! It was The Book. The Book made me do it!" He bawled loudly.

The rain got heavier, pelting onto the windshield so hard he thought it was going to smash. He couldn't take it anymore - he swerved his car. Straight for the hill. Yet, a tree stopped his car and he was yanked forward from the brutal impact.

Blood dripped down from his nose, and he swiped it away quickly. He couldn't kill himself. George was at home. His sweet little boy. His innocent little boy. He grabbed his head and began to sob ferociously. He loved George so much. Why did he even consider that, he couldn't leave his only son alone.

Elijah slowly began to reverse out of the wreckage that he had just made, tears still dripping quickly out of his eyes. George. That's all he kept thinking of as he made his way home. George.

The rickety car pulled up outside of the house, slowing to a stationary position and Elijah stepped out, slamming the door behind him. Not bothering with the clean up of his blood-filled boot. He dragged his hands down his face, smearing his tears and blood, trying to hide the fact that he had been crying.

He looked over to the window that showed the inside of the living room and there sat George. His Georgey. He was still sat there playing on his game - engrossed in whatever he was doing. Walking up to the door, he took a deep breath before turning the knob and opening it up.

The sweet homely aroma of the Carter home filled his nostrils. He looked over at the mess of the kitchen and slammed the door shut, putting it to the back of his mind.

He strolled into the living room, and looked at George. George looked away from his game and smiled at Elijah. His toothy mouth showing.

He had recently lost a couple of teeth and it was the cutest thing ever. He stood up off the sofa, and placed his controller carefully on the arm rest. He ran up to Elijah and hugged him tightly. Elijah hugged back just as tight and whispered in George's ear "I love you George, " He whispered, soothingly. He hugged him more tightly than ever before. His eyes began leaking of salty tears again. "Oh, George. I love you so much."

Chapter 3

The City of Cairo

As they landed, Elijah saw the grand, ancient pyramids in the warm, bustling desert far in the distance. He was relieved to finally be off of the plane, but was overwhelmed by the wave of heat that suddenly hit his already sweaty face. Although it was late at night, the airport was full with people waiting in line to show their passports to security. When he got out of this line, he retrieved his suitcase and hailed a taxi to his hotel.

The following morning, Elijah dragged himself out of his comfortable bed, still tired from the day before. He brushed his teeth, got changed into his inadequate attire and made his way downstairs for breakfast. After he had finished eating his breakfast, he caught a taxi to the ancient temple.

Elijah was greeted with a long line of tourists, who were eagerly awaiting there visit to the temple. Elijah was no exception, he too was eager to get inside and explore. He loved the views from the outside, the sloped sandstone walls and the statue of some old Egyptian pharaoh. But this waiting was giving Elijah a sense of impatience and anger and he felt like pushing through the populous queue.

Finally, Elijah had had enough, so he wandered off to a shaded area with no tourists, completely oblivious to the 'restricted area' signs that were positioned along the grainy sandstone walls alongside the what seemed to be thousands of scorpions scurrying up the walls.

After a while in the shade, Elijah decided to step outside into the sweltering desert and take in the views of the ancient temple from the outside. Whilst he was admiring the view of the decrepit yet beautiful temple he saw something that caught his eye. It was a book. An old worn leather book, with streaks of opulent gold running through it. But something felt weird. Elijah was drawn to this book by what seemed to be some sort of connection - it was like he was meant to find it. He slowly, but not hesitantly, approached the book, he then picked it out of the soft, grainy sand where it was positioned.

Despite enduring the blistering heat within the City of Cairo, Elijah still managed to jostle his way through the dry and untrodden deserts, barely making it to his hotel room. As drained as the middle aged doctor was, he still was intrigued to read what the book had held for him.

As Elijah opened the book, he suddenly felt a

dark feeling rush over him, a surge of energy going towards his brain with no control over anything. Symbols were flying through his brain, the only feeling he could feel was vulnerability.

He started to feel light-headed as something came upon him, like he had a second consciousness. He felt like he was being manipulated by a foreign presence, like something had control over him. He felt weak and dizzy. He felt powerful, full of energy, full of magic.

Chapter 4

St Dymphna

7 years later

Elijah stepped out of his car, the pure dread of nostalgia filled his head. His breath got caught in his throat but he brushed it off quickly.

"Got to keep it professional, " He muttered, deep breaths escaping his mouth. His shiny shoes clicked on the pavement as he walked up to the main doors of his workplace: St. Dymphna Hospital for the Criminally Insane.

A plastered smile was quickly smacked onto his face as he approached the building. The receptionist smiled fondly at him as he passed. His white lab coat falling behind him as he stalked through the corridors.

He reached his main office, with a gold plaque sat proudly on his door: DR. CARTER. Turning the matching golden knob, he looked through the frosted glass to see a dark figure standing inside. Hesistantly, he opened the door - only to be greeted by an empty room.

Sighing, he walked to his desk and plopped his belongings in his drawer, as well as dropping his leather briefcase on the carpeted floor. Elijah sat on his chair, resting his hands on his eyes. Daydreaming. Thinking.

A knock disrupted his thinking, and in walked Daniel with a large set of keys in his hand.

"Ready for the rounds?" Daniel questioned,

swinging the keys on his index finger around in circles, slightly whistling a tune. Elijah hummed in response, checking his watch before stepping up from his chair. 9:04.

He put his charming, commercial smile on his wrinkled face and left his office with Daniel. The occasional beeps of the security cards being used rung in his ears.

The click of shoes echoed through the endless corridors of the hospital. The hospital corridors all looked the same. The same windows. The same benches dotted occasionally around the building. The same odd plant in corners of the tedious blue painted walls. The only thing that was different was the patients in each room.

Their first stop was Clara.

Daniel was speaking to Clara, a young, alluring girl, who was sent here when she was only sixteen for the murder of her parents. A brutal murder because her parents had forced her to move from her home in Australia, to England to get help with her illnesses. Her schizophrenia. Daniel peered over at Elijah who was stood in the corner of her room, who seemed to be in deep conversation with somebody. Yet - nobody was speaking to him. Speaking to nobody but himself. Hushed whispers came from his mouth, and pauses as if he was receiving an answer.

"Dr. Carter!" Daniel shouted quietly. "Focus, please, " Elijah looked up at Daniel, nothing behind his eyes until something changed. Like a switch in his brain.

"Sorry Dr. Larson. I was daydreaming!" he laughed, his wrinkles showing even more as he did so. Daniel pressed his lips together in an attempt of a smile as he helped Clara back into her bed.

They made their way back into the endless corridors, onto their next patient.

The two doctors now only had one more patient to do. Brooke. Brooke was the oldest patient in the hospital. She was sent here after the loss of her two sisters. She claimed she could still hear them in her head. Everyday. Her family, couldn't cope with her craziness anymore and sent her away.

Upon arriving in Brooke's room, a shrewd look was fired at Elijah. If looks could kill, Elijah would most definitely be dead. Daniel repeated the same questions to Brooke as he asked Clara. Elijah seemed happier than he was before Daniel snapped at him. Chirpier. He was humming as he checked Brooke's room for any contraband items. Tapping his foot occasionally to his odd tune.

Daniel glanced over at at Elijah weirdly, before making sure Brooke was okay before they left. Elijah took his glasses off and put it in the top pocket of his lab coat, suddenly waltzing off to his office.

Daniel flashed a smile towards Brooke before stropping off to find Louise. "I'm sick and tired of all his craziness. He's driving me up the wall, " he muttered as he made his way to the art room where Louise would most likely be. He barged the door open ducking as he entered - his tall 6'9 frame not fitting through the door. He quickly scanned the room before beginning his rant.

"Elijah is driving me up the wall!" He chants,

pacing around the room. Watching how Louise carefully stroked her canvas with her paint brush. With each stroke, she smiled as the blue colour she was using became more prominent on the white canvas.

"He's rambling to himself constantly, he's insane!" He exclaimed, stopped pacing and looked at Louise's painting.

"That's really good, Lou." He says suddenly. She looks up from her painting and blushes.

"Thank you, Daniel." She mumbles.

Elijah erupted through the door, locking the door behind him and chucking the keys onto the desk. They slid against the polished wood and stopped luckily when they reached the edge.

He sat down on his cushioned seat and began spinning around in circles. He opened up the drawer and grabbed the leather bound book. Opening it up, a puff of smoke emitted from the book, flipping pages on its own.

He sat in his office for hours, staring at the limitless pages of the book. Daniel knocked on the door multiple times, and each time somebody knocked, he threw something at the door. Glass shards and debris were scattered throughout the room, creating a hazard to anybody who dared to walk in.

Nothing seemed to break his gaze from the book. Not even the screaming of the patients. Not even the footsteps of pacing doctors. Not even the clock chiming eleven. The sun had set and the stars had begun aligning themselves precariously in the sky.

His lamp flickered on and off as he stared aimlessly at The Book. The Book which he couldn't read. It was full of hireoglyphics and he couldn't understand a single word that was indented in the book.

Yet, he couldn't look away.

Chapter 5

The Way Back

As the clock on Elijah's wrist clicked slowly - so did his patience. The common question recurred over in his head a thousand times, "What could the book do for me?" He leaned back in his chair, putting his newly shined shoes upon the desk and hands behind his head. It felt like he was slowly but surely driving himself to insanity. The room was surrounded by dimly lit lights, which gave a more uncomfortable, eerie feeling to the room. Elijah's eyes fixated on the book in front of him. It then became clear - he needed assistance. This wasn't the kind of ordeal he could pull off himself.

As the sky grew dark, a low mist of smog etched over the horizon. Elijah glanced at the book, then back at his pen. Then an idea came over him - a moment of realisation. In his old university there was a student named Nancy Smith, that he saw in a newspaper once. She studied hieroglyphics, or so as he remembered. Duplicity was a common attribute to Elijah's personality - he needed this.

As the roaring engine revved forward: nothing else could be heard but the loud shrieking thunder. The old road was just as he remembered it, same old same old. He shifted his eyes to the radio and turned it to 'Classical music FM', a station he throughly enjoyed. And he continued down the road of nostalgia - he became apparent of the endless possibilities of the book and its power: which was neatly placed in the passenger seat.

As the raging storm continued, Elijah continued to drive on and finally reached his destination: 'Stanford University' as the sign read out before the car park. As the door slammed shut, Elijah felt the adrenaline rushing through him. Each step made him feel closer to his goal - his achievement. But maybe it wouldn't go to plan, "What if she wanted the book for herself? What if she lied to me? What if she wasn't there?" he questioned, anxiously. He made his way through the damp corridor. Echoing whispers escaped the ceilings making the building feel compact. He told the receptionist, "I am looking for someone who can translate hieroglyphics? You see - I discovered this book a while ago, and heard there is someone here who can." The receptionist gave a shifty smile with a raised eyebrow, her pool blue eyes glancing over her glasses. "Let me get this right, Mr Carter? Previous student? You are still on our records, even after twenty years."

"That's correct, now I feel old, " he grumbled. The receptionist gave a careless nod.

"The public library, " she continued on, "On your left then-"

"I know where to go." He interrupted.

Hazy, serene, ideal: whirling wind peered through the cracks of the broken windows, echoing through the foyer. Silence echoed around the interior of the damp walls, caving in slowly. As he turned the doorknob of the weakened wooden door, there appeared a girl sitting silently. "Nancy?" he called out.

A peculiar expression was painted across her stern face. "Yes?" she responded and she thought to herself, "At this time of night?"

Elijah explained the book and its origin, leaving out his unspeakable intention of what he had in mind to do with it. Nancy was almost overwhelmed with this opportunity - the opportunity that was rare and now she could put her skills into work. A grin gleamed across her face and she took the book from his hands, Elijah watching cautiously.

A feeling of uncertainty passed Nancy like a gust of wind. As she peered through the contents etched across the page in fine writing, she couldn't help but find them strange. Nancy began murmuring to herself, "Whose hands this may end up in, " she continued, "Should understand the fate of what happens next..." She glanced back and Elijah, then back to the book. In a confused state of mind, she continued to translate the next couple of pages. The book was compelling and enswirled the atmosphere with ill-fitting thoughts. "I can't thank you enough for this - I don't think you've realised what you have done for me, " Elijah disclosed.

"Not a problem." she spoke, jolted.

Afterwards, Elijah clenched the book in his hands and made his way to his plan for destruction. The more he stepped, the more a grin etched across his face. Creaking slowly, then the door made a BANG! It was frail - the university wasn't anything new. She glared upon hours upon hours of work that she had to complete - a sigh passed through her silently. Now nothing but cloudy thoughts left Nancy alone in the library, her thoughts anxious...

Chapter 6

Pain of The Past

The rising sun casted a warm hue through the open windows of her apartment on the 4th floor. There was no need for an alarm clock this morning since it was Thursday, one of Lisa's days off besides Sunday, yet she still woke up early. As much as she wished she could stay in and avoid the disappointment from her family, Lisa had to visit her sister before she went insane, even more than she already was.

Her arms stretched above her head and toes curled the other end letting out a wince of pain from the aching that her job blessed her with the night before. Sighing, she lethargically dragged her feet out of bed, placing them into her light purple slippers.

She reached her front door smothered in posters and a calendar with Thursday ticked on every week of every month. Amongst the collage was a bare spot. On the floor was a family portrait of her, Clara and their parents. Lisa grabbed the photo and held it to her chest. A tear already forming in her eye she sighed "I'm sorry, it wasn't her, I wish you could understand"

She wiped her tears and left the house, walking to the train station.

She took the train at around 12:07. The sun rays still shining through the windows, heating up the unoccupied vinyl seats. She placed her purse on her lap as she settled down for the 30 minute journey ahead. Resting her head against the window, she stared into the city slowly turning into rural land. Cities turned into villages, skyscrapers turned into hills and crowds turned into the odd dog walker.

Her black converse tapped on the floor as she leaped off of the train into the countryside. Amongst the lush green valleys sat a large brick structure, completely dulling the atmosphere. A sign displaying St Dymphna Mental Institute stood proudly in front of the building.

A smile was plastered on her face, masking the dread that crowded her thoughts, as she stepped foot into the building. She situated herself amidst a desert of chairs, she was the only one visiting today. "Lisa Clark here to see Clara Clark" a doctor announced through the speakers. She rose from her seat and dawdled through the corridors, slumping her back wishing the ward could go on some sort of lockdown and give her an excuse to escape the bitter fragrance of bleach.

After the eternity of corridors she entered Clara's ward. 11. The disparity in smell from the corridors to her feminine sweet room hit Lisa like a splash of cold water.

She sat beside Clara, the plastered on beaming smile slowly disintegrating off of her face. The awkwardness between the two was never settled, but nevertheless Lisa visited as much as she could. Lisa's eyes gazed accross the ward, avoiding eye contact between the two. The walls were painted an oyster white and the sweet jasmine scent lingered off of them. It was rather boring despite Clara's charming taste in interior design.

Breaking the silence Lisa exhaled "Do you miss them?"

"Who?" Clara questioned not breaking her straight face

"Our parents."

Lisa sat back in her chair, flooded with memories of the darkest portion of her mind.

"C, just try it, we're doing this for the benefit of you"

Clara had just got back from school. Slamming the door behind her. Infront of her were her parents sitting at the kitchen table, head in their hands. Startled by the slam, Clara's mother dragged her hands down her face, her eyes nearly rolling out of the sockets.

"I am not going to some stupid therapy that's not even going to, not even going to help me!" she stuttered throwing her bag against the wall in full force. She barged past Lisa, stomping up the stairs.

"Clara, calm down, the floors going to cave through" Lisa muttered, her shoulders slumped, looking up through her long luscious eyelashes. Clara replied with a dirty look, scrunching her nose and shifting her eyes up and down Lisa's body.

Clara's hands were gripped tight. She was annoyed. The voices in her head were overwhelmingly loud: screaming at her, demanding her to do awful things or else she would be the one injured. The scent of rancid, out-of-date milk devoured the room. A glass cup smashed to pieces lay helplessly

43

on the floor. And the adrenaline rushed through Clara's arm. The realisation hit her, she just did that.

Her family burst through the door, a panic-stricken face painted upon them. Clara's mum had her phone raised to her ear. A low-pitched voice coming from the mobile: "St Dymphna's Mental Institute"

"You're sending me to a mental institute for the criminally insane?" Clara bellowed, clenching her hands by her side. Nobody replied and the room fell silent in awkwardness.

A large grin was smeared across her face, Clara slowly bent down, her back to her parents. She picked up a shard of glass from the plethora of pieces on her floor. Her hands bled from her tight grip. She stood up and turned around, the putrid milk smell was the least of her concerns. She walked towards her family with a content smile yet blood was dripping from behind her back leaving a trail of crimson stain on her carpet.

She walked closer and closer towards her par-

ents, removing her hands from behind her back she raised her hand to reveal a deep red waterfall of blood yet this wasn't the only pool of blood. Across her fathers neck was as a narrow opening, gushing with blood dyeing his light blue suit. The once silent room erupted into an echo of screams bouncing off the walls and a subtle choking in the background. Clara turned around to face her mother who was stationary in pure terror. Her pupils devouring her iris.

The same glass shard used to kill her father was now inserted inside the stomach of her mother. She twisted it inside of her causing her to continuously jolt forwards as a crimson juice spewed from her mouth. Clara never took her eyes off of her mother, watching every last second of her life.

Lisa remained in the room, her eyebrows were furrowed and her bottom lip quivering at the sight of her parents lay on the floor. Completely lifeless.

Lisa's eyes glazed with tears as she snapped back into the present with Clara sat infront of her.

"Not at all, " Clara smirked. She glared at the doctor and Lisa was escorted out of the room.

Chapter 7

Leo

The grey, faded walls of St Dymphna's Hospital for the Criminally Insane were driving Leo insane on this particular Tuesday morning. Nothing had seemed to be going his way on that day after all, everything was getting on his nerves. He just never said that things were getting on his nerves because of his social anxiety, which often overpowered and got the better of him.

Suddenly, a large group of people came rushing down the corridors, directly past Leo's room. Leo began to feel his face rush with blood, his hands began to tremor as he heard the footsteps come closer. Panicked, he rushed to his bed, attempting to hide his face, so that if the group looked through his gloomy, filthy window they wouldn't see him.

Eventually, the group passed his window, without staring in, which Leo was very thankful for. Once he felt it was safe to, he left the safety of his bed and went to his desk. He opened his multi-langual dictionary and attempted to learn a language that he hadn't heard the name of before.

As he sat there, skimming the pages of the Belarusian dictionary, he sat looking at the words. "Dziakui, " he repeated quietly, "Dziakui, Dz..ia..a..a..a " His words began to tremor. He couldn't pronounce how he usually could. A word had popped up in the dictionary. A word that sent his mind

flying back to the day of his childhood trauma.
The reason he was here in the first place. A day
that changed his life. The day his dad killed his
mum.

All of a sudden, his mind was teleported back
to his childhood. Back to his earliest memories
with his dad and mum. In particular, one memory stuck out. His dad was working in the gar-
den, preparing fire wood for cooking later in the
night. His dad had been diagnosed with bipolar a
few weeks prior. He had been struggling with it,
as his depressive episodes often made him overly
violent, and he often struggled to express his feelings. Because of this, he shot out in a burst of
rage, and threw his axe straight in the direction
of Leo's mother. After this, Leo's memory began
to get blurry, it was traumatic enough for him to
remember her death, let alone her screams.

His mind then travelled to a few years later,
sending him vivid memories of the pale grey doctors office he sat it one Wednesday afternoon. The
doctor's voice was slurred and difficult to under-

stand, but Leo could pick out the word 'bipolar'. He could see his own feelings playing out on his younger self's face. He began to shake and break down to tears. Leo often relived his traumatic memories, but this time it felt all too real to him.

Thankfully, his mind sent him back to his empty hospital room. He was lost for words. His face had gone an eerie pale colour and his veins ran an odd sort of green-blue, vividly rushing with blood. He gently closed his book, and without a word, pushed his chair away from his desk. He decided it would be best to go to bed, sleep was his way of escaping his troubled past. It was the only way he could skip forward the clock, and pretend he lived an untroubled life.

Chapter 8

Time to Shine

Louise was dressed in a vibrant suit as her brush smoothly painted down her nearly finished canvas in her petite office. Although she looked joyful, inside was a different matter. Paintings of tulips and roses filled her office walls whilst the sun was beaming in through her window. Pink silky cushions were scattered all over her room with her painting essentials neatly packed into a clear box by the side of her desk. Clear canvases were piled up behind her rose pink office chair waiting eagerly to be painted. Louise sat at her desk for hours on end working on her patient information sheets, her head filled with stress, confusion and depression. Painting for her was escapism as her patience went as quick as a bullet. Once it was fired, she couldn't get it back.

She calmly turned around in her chair and admired her pastel yellow tulips standing proudly on her window ledge. The tulips in her window inspired her to paint unique flowers, fuchsia pink and pastel yellow with a light blue background. Louise had always liked to stand out from her fellow doctors with her sense of dress style and artwork. With suffering from mental health herself, she liked to portray her personality through her choice of clothing and artistic skills. On the outside she looked strong, but actually she was suffering from serious depression and anxiety.

Louise painted her canvas with stress running around in her head, trying to escape every day life. She tried flooding her memory with nothing but positive thoughts, but an endless to-do list overtook her thoughts. She painted her flowers a way in which no one else could copy, her own masterpiece which would truly belong to her. Louise mixed her pastel colours gracefully with the tips of her beautifully painted marble nails hovering over the brush. As soon as she lifted the paintbrush up, the power was in her hands to inspire others.

Louise found serenity from painting and had always wanted to sell her work world wide but she had never felt confident enough to peruse her dream. She was sitting in her office with the sun gleaming through the windows which allowed her to stop for a split second and think. Memories rushed around her head, thinking of the last time that they had a professional journalist in to interview the patients. Although St Dymphna's covered all of the patients needs, there was a lot to fix regarding the interior. If a journalist came in, it might promote the hospital to get extra funding. She scrambled through her paperwork to find her notepad and pen, immediately brainstorming notes and ideas.

She quickly searched on her computer for excellent journalists in their local area and came across Dequation Dingleberry. Dequation was a recent graduate and had been scouted many times already but was yet to secure his first professional paid job. Louise dialled his number promptly into her phone and waited for an answer. The constant ringing of the phone made Louise anxious and tense, clenching her fists tightly on her chaotic desk preparing herself for no answer. But suddenly, out of no where, a hushed voice answered the phone.

'Hello, Dequation speaking!' Dequation spoke cautiously.

'Hi Dequation, my name is Louise and I am calling from St Dymphna's hospital. I have noticed that you have recently graduated and you have an amazing profile online. It would be an absolute honour if we could have you to come in and interview the art class patients, what are your thoughts?' Louise confidently said to him.

Dequation was overwhelmed with the offer and delightedly told her that he would come in as soon as she was ready. They both discussed dates over the phone and made an arrangement to have the interview as soon as possible. Louise was ecstatic as she ended the call. She later picked up and email from him:

Hello Louise,

Thank you very much for your offer earlier on today to report on the art class. I must make you aware that this is my first professional paid job and my reputation will rely on this interview.

I would like to come in approximately 1 hour before the interview to get set up if that works with you?

Thank you again

Dequation Dingleberry

Journalist

Dequation spent the week before the interview preparing, worrying and buzzing with excitement. Ten full sheets of paper later and he had finished his preparation.

Notes and questions flooded the paper ready for the important interview. Every night leading up to the interview he practised to his hearts content, eagerly hoping that this interview would shape his future career.

Finally the day came to report on the art class.

Louise confidently greeted Dequation at the reception and showed him around before the interview. He strolled through the darkened corridors, cautiously walking past the patients bedrooms. He got to the art class just in time for the interviews after his preparation.

This was his time to shine.

Chapter 9

A New Opportunity

Dequation wandered into the art class, into his first job offer. This brand new opportunity in front of him made his veins buzz with excitement. Despite the overwhelming excitement, this was also met with a significant amount of nerves. Nerves that stemmed from the potential of him ruining this chance.

A friendly face popped up in front of him.

"Hi, I'm Clara! What's your name? Are you here for the art class? I am so excited."

Dequation jerked backwards.

"...erm... hi, I'm Dequation." he replied in a stutter.

"I will try my best not to tear these art projects apart." Clara said flippantly.

Dequation was transported back into a time where he last felt loved. His parents had divorced thirty-eight years ago, yet the sadness Clara had created felt like it had happened that very morning. The separation and pain from his dad walking away was a scar that had never fully healed.

Dequation felt the bittersweet sensibility of the phone call that he would have to tell his mum about this great opportunity at the end of the art class, that was met by the sting of never being able to tell his dad. Making his mother happy made him happy and filled him with joy, knowing this he had the confidence to get back into the swing of things.

Dequation snapped out of the memories to greet Louise, adorned with a paint splattered apron. They both exchanged a smile and a handshake as she ushered Dequation towards a chair at the back of the art room.

Leo was sat at a table on his own, near to where Dequation had been seated.

He muttered under his breath, just loud enough for Dequation to become suspicious.

"The book.. The book."

"Hi, I'm Dequation Dingleberry, I'm reporting the ward. Who are you?"

"Oh, hi, I'm, erm. I'm Leo." he kept his eyes on the table.

"What book are you talking about.. Liam. Sorry, Le-"

"Nothing! Noth.. No book." Leo returned, not letting Dequation finish his sentence.

Louise called the patients over, ready to begin the class. Dequation made notes towards the report as the paint was being splattered, each in different ways by the deviants of St Dymphna's.

Then, he noticed something.

During their earlier conversation, Louise had dropped her key card. The room was emptying. Surely she wouldn't notice if Dequation wandered around for a bit? Just to help with the report, of course.

He picked up the card, a new opportunity, and slipped it into his pocket.

He had a thought.

"Louise please may I go to the toilet please?"

"Yes, of course you can, just down the corridor to the left." Louise said with a smile on her face.

Cautiously, Dequation made his way down the corridor, past the toilets and towards the heart of the ward.

With the keycard in his hand, he thought of his mother, wondering whether she would appreciate what he was doing.

Dequation used the key card to explore the

heart of the wards as he walked down the corridor. He could hear a quiet voice in a foreign language. Unnervingly, down the corridor, the sound of banging echoing off the walls, he didn't dare go any deeper into the ward for his own sake, as he didn't want to risk getting caught and losing his job.

Chapter 10

Dingleberry's Antics

Dequation, as eager as he was, placed the key-card in a discreet location inside of his pocket and quickly embarked on his short journey throughout the endlessly long corridors. As he continued walking through the corridors, he could not help but feel as if the walls were closing in. They were damp, dusty white - probably hadn't been painted for decades.

Dequation was frantically speed walking through the endless corridors, like he had seen a ghost, scared for his life, and his mother's. These thoughts ran through his troubled mind endlessly, and these thought made him feel anxious and alone.

The ambience felt eerie to Dequation which worried him more. As he turned around the sharp, twisted corner, echoes of uneasiness ran through his mind. Pacing steadily, he reminded himself to think as positively as possible in this situation.

He was walking rapidly to try and find the book but walked a short distance through the door that said 'WAIT' and turned back around to look inside the window.

He considered if that was the right room that the book would be in.

He stared at the book for a short amount of time pondering if it was worth the risk to collect it.

Soon enough, he came to the realisation that the entire ward was full of perculiar people. Maybe it was just a simple book? Time wasn't on his side, so he took the risk and slowly but surely collected the book and wandered off to a discreet room.

As he was making his way to a discreet location, he surpassed a door that caught his attention. The door was different to the others. It was as if it hadn't been touched in a while. The keycard slot was unalike the other slots. It was unique in a sort of way. Dequation abruptly reached for his card to unlock the door however it didn't work. He tried again but again there was no luck. He pushed his sweaty face upon the large, stained glass peering for an entrance to the room; the only entrance was the door.

Dequation stepped back from the door to look at it. Above the door read '*LIBRARY* which was plastered with plastic symbols. The door was a frost, white colour with a small window placed on the top of it. Dequation tried the keycard one more time and it worked.

"Oh now it works, " Dequation murmured to himself in frustration. The door squeaked open with little effort which was unexpected. Dequation squeezed through the door and shut it despite the echoing noise. The smell of old books instantly overwhelmed his nose which resulted in him covering his nose in a quick reflex. The cold air from the library brushed across his face in a swoosh. Dequation stepped inside the library with caution, scouting the area. The shelves, which had the vast amount of books, looked as if they had rarely been used, washed with dust. Dequation pushed the door with the slightest bit of effort and it closed. *Maybe it had been used recently.* As Dequation made his way towards the circular, beige table, he placed the mysterious book on it and quickly scanned it. Midway through scanning the book, light, abrupt footsteps emerged from the corridors. Reflexively, Dequation left the library without looking back.

As Dequation ran through the short, cornered corridors, the sweat poured down his face while his chins jiggled through the motion. Through each turn he surpassed, the more tired he grew and eventually, he came to a stop where he checked his surroundings and came to realisation that he had forgot the book..

Chapter 11

Overtaken

The library was one of the largest rooms in the building - and yet it was always seemed to be so empty. The books sat untouched on the oak bookshelves, gathering dust as nobody really visited or read such poorly maintained books. Leo clicked through the wooden floor, his shoes squeaking with each step. The sound of his light steps echoed throughout the vast library, whilst Leo glanced over at the books. He had read hundreds of the books in this library, and still there was more to read. Running his fingers along the spines of books, craning his neck diagonally as he read each one. He knew the majority of languages, but he still wanted to find out more about the ancient Egyptian language.

He continued stepping through the long aisle, making his way to the back of the room where he hid his Egyptian language book secretly - he didn't want anybody to take it. He needed to learn this language.

Finally arriving at the back bookshelf, he picked up the book and flipped to the dog-eared page, continuing to read from where he left off last night (before he was ushered to bed by Dr Larson).

A word stopped him in his tracks. The word: Mut. He continued to read on which told him that it was a goddess which translates to Mother. A gut-wrenching feeling attacked his insides as he

read the small paragraphs several times. Mother.
Mother. Mother.

He ripped that page from the book, crumpling
it up and throwing it harshly at a nearby wall. It
reminded him too much of his past. Too much
of the axe being thrown at her. Too much of the
glassy eye that looked at Leo for the last time.
Too much of his Father's cruel laughter, sending
chills down his spine.

As Leo was reading the paragraph in his head
over and over again the pain grew worse and worse.
Tears filled his eyes because of that horrific thing
that happened to her. Only sadness ran through
Leo's body, blaming himself for the death of his
Mother. Maybe he could have done something
to stop his fathers unforgivable actions? His only
wish that he could speak to his mother at least
one more time.

Stomping through the aisles, he stood on the
crumpled ball that he threw at the wall previously and slumped down on the floor. Hugging
his knees, he was crying like a child trying to re-

mind himself that he has to stay positive. The only thing on his mind was his beautiful, loving Mother, and how much she meant to him. The only feeling he felt was the hatred towards his Father.

BANG!

Something hit the floor - something large. It came from the wooden table covered with dust. Leo whipped his head around jumping out of his skin, looking at the cause of the noise. A large leather-bound book had dropped onto the floor, a plume of dust and smoke arising around it. The book was streaked with lavish gold symbols - ones which Leo could not understand. The leather was charred at the sides as if it had been in the fiery pits of hell and the oxidised pages stuck out like a sore thumb in contrast to the deep brown coloured book.

As Leo looked more intensely, he realised that the streaks of sumptuous gold were actually the Eye of Horus, indented delicately on it. He stood up quickly, the bookcase shaking from the force of his abruptness. Leo stalked up to the book, bending over cautiously, peering at the book. The Book, all of a sudden, began flicking through the pages on its own. Dust billowed out, making Leo splutter and cough. Covering his mouth, he stepped back quickly waiting for it to end.

The Book stopped flicking, stopping at a certain page. Without moving his feet, he elevated his neck so he could peer at what page it had landed on. A page full of hieroglyphs. He could only make out a few words, so he picked it up - shocked by the heaviness of it. As it hit the table, even more dust flew out from underneath it, causing Leo to splutter even more.

His eyes scanned against the symbols, recognising them but not being able to decipher them fully. Although, he was able to make out a few words: Dark and Magic. He slammed the book shut quickly, but something felt different inside of him. Something odd.

A voice entered his head, a deep voice. It sounded like an old man speaking. Luckily, it was in English, but the speaker seemed to have a distinct foreign accent.

"Join me, " It was a husky voice, "Join me and we can rule this land beyond." His head began to spin and he tried standing up using the support of the bookshelf. The bookshelf snapped and he fell further down again. He began crawling towards his room, trying his hardest to regain self control of his own body.

Chapter 12

The King of Kings

Deep within the pits of hell, through the blood-born fires, the musty clouds of ashen grey smog faded over the afterlife. Ramesses stood tall, a defining figure emerging through the fallen mist, which laid at the bottom of his ankles. Fire bit at his ankles like a bush of thorns, entwining itself around his body and creeping into his mind, giving him horrible hallucinations of his time of death.

The atmosphere in hell was empty, no happiness could be felt throughout the afterlife after all, only depression, desperation, and disgust. Rameses knew that he deserved better. He was the King of Kings, everyone knew that. He was the most celebrated pharaoh ever, the pharaoh that changed Egypt, one to be remembered forever. He deserved the very best, better than heaven, better than what God has. He was God.

Suddenly, a strange feeling stirred from inside of him. A feeling of life, of power, of glory. It ran throughout his veins, spread to his head, alerting his brain, sending electrical shocks throughout him. He racked his mind to think of a reason for this feeling, a sensation this brilliant was rare in hell, almost impossible.

After what seemed like many hours of figuring

76

out what the feeling was, he knew. It surely had to be. There was nothing else left that could provide him this alive feeling, nothing but the book.

He sat tall in his throne, confidence pouring out of him, knowing he would be back in the over world soon. He laughed in satisfaction, knowing he had won, nobody could stop him now. He had lost some battles but this was the war and he was not prepared to lose it now. The game of life was his, he truly was the king of kings.

Chapter 13

The Realisation

Quietly, George snuck into Elijah's office. He wasn't initially searching for anything, he had just wanted some time with his dad. After all, his dad had seemed very distant. George had known that his dad was going through a hard time, and he had never been particularly fond of his dad, but he still wanted some quality time with him.

Suddenly, George remembered that his dad had kept a photobook with all the photos of George and his mum. His dad often didn't talk about his mum, George assumed that it was because his dad never truly missed his mum. All of a sudden, he stumbled across an aged, leather book. It was a book he had never seen before, with a gold, shining eye of Horus. As soon as he saw it, he knew who to go to. He had to find her. He had to find Nancy.

He hurried out the book into his bag, being careful not to bend the pages, and ran out to the canteen, as he knew Nancy was on her lunch. He began to speed-walk, not wanting others to know he was getting faster with every step.

Finally, after two minutes of awkward speed-walking, he found Nancy, eating her signature chicken Caesar salad as always. He rushed to sit opposite her, and carefully pulled out the book. It had a subtle glow to it, as if it was something of an ancient myth or legend.

"What the hell is that?" questioned Nancy, confused as to why George had pulled out Elijah's book.

"Nancy, I found this in Dad's drawer, do you know anything about it?" responded George, hoping that Nancy's knowledge of egyptology comes in to hand.

"Well, thats the book that I translated for your Dad a few weeks back, but I never got the chance to fully do it, I could try and translate it again if you want?" asked Nancy, hoping George would say yes as the book had always interested her.

"If you could, I know your on your lunch but it could help us find out more about the weird behaviour of some of the patients" replied George.

Nancy nodded her head, and began to write down ideas on her nearby notepad. At the start, she couldn't find anything of too much interest, mainly commonly known Egyptian myths and the aftermath of ancient Egyptian legends, commonly known stuff to a well traversed egyptolgy student.

81

After reading through and educating George on some common folk tales, a specific story came up. One that not many historians know about. The story of Ramesses II. As the legend goes, Rameses was a great and intelligent pharaoh, a war lord of ancient Egypt, leading the empire to great successes in war. However, he had been too boastful in his life, and was now stuck in the afterlife, left with no surviving remains on earth, apart from a ruined statue in his birth town Aswan and a book that published his story.

"George, hear me out here, in Egyptian legend the way for a pharaoh to come back to the over-world is to have a surviving relic in the overworld. Since his statue had been destroyed, his relic was the book. There is only one book on his story, and that book is infront of us right now, " said Nancy timidly, as she now understood just how much power she had given Elijah.

"Nancy, I'm sorry if I am appearing stupid, but how does this relate to my dad?" George questioned, but upon noticing Nancy's timid face, he gently picked up her hand in an effort to comfort her.

"No George, you don't sound stupid, but this book must have overtaken your dad, and Rameses is using your dad and St Dymphna's as a way to get into the overworld, " spoke Nancy, whilst sounding panicked. George was silent for a moment, had his dad really been possessed by an ancient pharaoh?

"Well if you are right, and the book does truly overtake people, why haven't we been overtaken?" asked George.

"Lets make a list, it may sound stupid, but it makes the most sense, " said Nancy, in hope that her and George would figure out something. George nodded his head, and they began to figure out a list. They wrote down all of the known possessed people, and everything that they had in common. After about 10 minutes of constant debating, they finally settled on something. The possessed people all had a mental illness.

They stared at their results in shock. How had

83

this even gotten in Elijah's possession in the first place?

Chapter 14

The Sane

Dim, serene, vacant: the library seemed empty to Brooke, as thoughts clouded her judgement. She needed to read, to clear her head. As she entered through the door, glances from other doctors made her weary. Each step she took felt judged. As the longest patient, it was expected for her to be even remotely insane. She was not however - and she dreamed of the days where she could finally escape. Brooke's feet urged forwards towards to row of books named 'Travel'. She glanced excitedly.

As Brooke searched for a book worth reading, her finger felt the back of each book. Well-made, woven or broken. She wondered how many chances she would get to visit these places. The chances of any travel happening remained low. Brooke's stomach churned just thinking about this, but she thought, "What could I possibly do?" She continued to trek slowly until the row ended. Around the other side was a short row of books, it was a limited selection of course.

She reached for a book, a crimson red edge - with clear blue skies and palm trees dotted amongst the horizon. The sea was clear and a colourful sea of fish could be seen. The book title read: 'Santorini: a biography'. Brooke raised an eyebrow, unintentionally. Jealously was never an emotion Brooke felt - but in this moment however, she couldn't help it. She glared at the pale walls, high ceilings, barred windows. Was this a place that she could be staying at for the forseeable future? Even though it felt like a lifetime already. The walls lacked creation and the room was mostly empty. The only part of the room that felt remotely similar was the arm chair in the corner of the room, and that was with no pillow or stool.

As her shaky feet edged further, followed by utter silence, she entered the array of books that read 'History section'. She ran her fingers through the side of the novels - but this time quicker, and did not give too much thought into it. Until one - a brown, old, with fine carvings stuck out to her. Her hand etched for this book and pulled out to reveal an eye, one that she was unfamilar with. Brooke grasped the book in both of her hands. It was strangely alluring - so she walked over to the uncomfortable armchair in the corner to read.

Brooke's curiosity peaked as she had never seen a book with such unique design - light purple lines etched over the book. Arabic writing was delicate over the ancient-looking book. Although it had a lovely design - the question was clear in Brooke's head: why was a book that wasn't in the same language in the Pysch hopsital? Maybe there were some highly intelligent patients? With no regrets, Brooke opened onto the first page. Bizarre - smooth writing edged over the page like the notes of a song. She couldn't understand a word of it, and her mind was already cloudy. Brooke closed the ancient book and placed it on the side of the armchair. She couldn't quite grasp the strange ideal of the book. The book remained on the side of the chair - with almost a strange feeling surrounded it, like it was literal. Brooke wanted to make the most out of this rare visit, so she forced herself to inspect the other array of books.

Creaking slowly, the door etched open. There appeared Alexander Blakley with a smiling glare, but nothing behind the eyes. But apart from this inescapable fact, he presented himself in a way which consisted of only confidence - something rare within a patient at a mental institute. Ever since he entered the room, an uncomfortable atmosphere filled the room like a disease. With a swing in his step, he walked over to the carefully arranged books cautiously inspecting each one. The doctors dark glare could not change the way Alex felt - he simply did not care. Within the plain library, some books were banned such as horror and crime. The closest Alex could get to crime would be the mystery books, another pile of short collections. Alex closely analysed the books that appeared to him.

Out of the etches of Blakely's curiosity, he glanced over at the book laying across the armchair. A librarian was about to pick up the book until he muttered,

"Hey can I look at that?"

Alex's patience was slipping slowly - just like his mask that he had made for himself. The librarian nodded and swiftly gave the book to Alex. As he clenched the book in his hands, an eerie atmosphere crept over him. Carefully analysing the ancient book's title, he felt as if he understood.

As almost if he spoke the language!

Even if this book appeared to have ancient heritage, it looked almost perfectly preserved. The edges of the page were not crumpled - nor did the colours seem less colourful. Alex was confused - but he did not let this distract him and he continued to search through the contents of the book. The writing of old all seemed apparent now. He began to zone out - pupils becoming smaller and the feeling of zoning out. A book that used to be normal moments ago now resulted in twisted fate. Then, the book slipped from his hand and fell onto the floor with the thud of a gunshot. The sanity of Alex Blakely slipped. A cold, stern stare of a true sociopath broke through the cracks of his appearance. With his arms by his side, and a face drained of emotion, he stepped forward with a steady pace. It was almost as if he was looking for something - or someone. Silent muttering could be heard escaping from Alexander. A creaking of the door handle, and a slam of a door left the library in silence.

Bright, alluring sunshine crept through the cracks of the window frame into the library. Brooke silently expressed her concern for the sudden situation, but she decided to keep out of it: mostly for her own safety, especially since it involved Alex. The question now prolonged itself - what could that book have possibly done to him?

"I shouldn't, I shouldn't get involved." Brooke muttered under her breath. But the eerie glow slipping from the contents of the twisted book furthered her curiosity and she couldn't help but stare. Now she could only feel the concern etching over her like a cape.

Chapter 15

Red Handed

It was a dull and cold day, so the idea of going into the library was appealing. It was empty so he took advantage of it. He was walking around, looking at all the books trying to find one that looked good enough for him. Thoughts were circling around his head so he decided to pick a book and stick with it to try and take his mind off the thoughts and voices. He was looking through the many rows of books to try and find one he took a liking to but nothing was interesting to Jamie. He wandered around for a bit longer trying to find something to his taste, but still couldn't find anything. He decided to go down the 'history' section just to see if there was anything else. As he was walking down the long line of books, dismay filled his head. He was going to give up looking, but something caught his eye.

He walked over to the end of the row because he saw a book hanging off the side of the shelf, it was the only book not in line so he went over. This was one particular book that stood out to Jamie. "When did this book get here, I've never seen it before?" he said to himself confused. He ran his hand across the shelf and picked up the book. It was a brown book, it look very old and worn out. Jamie took it off the shelf and admired the book wondering if he should read it to not. He took a liking to the book so after back and forth with himself he decided to read it.

Jamie read the book and immediately started to act off. "That was weird, " he said under his breath. Then out of no where he started feeling really irritated. His body went tense and his stomach was crawling. He just brushed it off and went to read a different book. As he was looking for a different book he couldn't stop thinking about that one particular book which was causing his mind to run wild. "You should kill.." the voices in his head said. Jamie tried to keep the voices quiet and stop them from dominating his head, like what the doctors would tell him. But the voices were too powerful and it got to the point where he couldn't take it anymore.

Jamie darted out the library, too slow to be running but too fast to be walking. He turned the corners of the hallways. He was out of breath but he still kept quick on his feet. Thoughts were spinning round his head at a million miles an hour, he didn't know what to do with himself but he managed to keep himself calm so no one questioned it.

As he was walking around the hallways he started to think about that book he found in the library, for some reason it couldn't leave his mind. He was still flying round the corners of the hallways trying to find someone, trying to find something.

As he went round one more corner he spotted Alex. He ran to Alex and asked him many questions. "Alex have you read the book?" "do you know anything about it?" Jamie said flooding Alex with questions.

"Yes I have read the book, it made my body crawl and I'm not feeling right, " Alex says with a blank look on his face.

"What do we do now then?" Jamie says in a angry tone. Jamie was getting flashbacks off the past because of the book. Every little thing was triggering the memories for Jamie so because of that it was filling his mind with more and more rage. He needed to do somthing to take this rage out. He had an idea.

They both looked at eachother and it was almost like they read each others mind. They moved swiftly down the corridor. Looking for something along the lines of a weapon, something they could do damage with. They moved room to room trying to look for something, then they found that one of the staff had left a door open. It was dead silent, not a single soul to be heard or seen. They slowly walked into the open room and scanned it. They saw that there was a knife in one of the draws that got left open. The shine of the sharp blade drew their attention. Alex stood by the door to see if someone was there "You've got to be fast I don't think we have much time to do this" Alex said with a worried tone. Jamie moved hastily and picked it up.

"I've got it, let's go!" Jamie said. They quickly closed the draw and moved away from the room with the sharp, shining knife.

Jamie and Alex started moving quickly down the corridor to try and find someone who would be their target. They went down the corridor and turned right down the hallway where all the patients went, but it was empty. It was so quiet you could hear the wind howling through the windows. As they were about to leave the corridor they hear shuffling from behind them. They started moving in direction towards the patient. When they got close enough Jamie started to get the knife out discreetly so the patient wouldn't know. As they walked past then they stabbed his back three times, the blood curdling screams and the glass breaking shouts of the patient filled the corridor but no one was around. His face immediately turned paper white as he dropped down into the floor. A pool of blood started to spread along the hallway floor. Seconds later he screamed his last scream and took his last breath. Alex and Jamie stood there, frozen watching the patient slowly and painfully die. Worried that they were going to get caught Jamie and Alex didn't stay for long after that.

They saw that they did their plan perfectly and they were happy it worked out. "Come on we need to leave incase someone comes and sees us here." Jamie said with a very low tone. They ran away leaving the dead patient laying there on the floor with no regets, not feeling bad, no emotions. They just ran off around all the corners like nothing had ever happened.

Chapter 16

Call for Help

Dequation began to realise that the ward was not as it initially seemed. He had seen some strange things at the hospital, but a murder surely topped them all. This really confused and worried Dequation, he knew that he had to get this story out to the world. This would be the story that made his career, it had to be.

He began to set off to the only place he knew could help him, the office. He could use the computer to alert the outside world. He could alert the police. Maybe even put himself forward for a medal of recommendation from the mayor, as after all he would have saved an entire hospital. Most importantly, this could be the story to send him straight to success. His previously shortcoming career could be changed, he just had to get to the office. He began to sprint as fast as he could, faster then ever before, around the maze-like corridors of St Dymphna's Hospital for the Criminally Insane.

Meanwhile, Dr Daniel Larson was relaxing in the break room, sighing heavily as he had just gotten back from doing rounds, and decided that he wanted a break. A whirring sound began filling the sound of his office as the coffee machine began filling his cup. Frothing with each spurt of brown liquid energy. When suddenly a rush of footsteps filled his ears. Assuming it was just a patient, his sigh was irritated and he swung open the door - squinting his eyes as he peered out into the distance of the long hallway.

A blurred outline. A tall figure. Heading closer and closer towards Daniel.

Daniel rushed to Dr Louise Johnson's office, having all access to all of the security cameras he thought it was wise to do so. Dequation looked up from his fast-moving feet, noticing the sound of a door slamming. Dr Larson had rushed from his room, sprinting to Dr Louise Johnson's room.

Dequation got closer and closer towards the office. His eyes were practically pound signs as he thought of all not the money he could earn from this story. All of the fame. All of the popularity. He smiled cheekily to himself, nearing to the office.

Daniel finally reached Louise's door, and began rapidly knocking on until she let him in.

"Louise!!" he exclaimed, "Louise! Come Quick! Someone is running to the office!"

Louise quickly gathered herself and set of running with Daniel.

Louise and Daniel began to start sprinting towards the mysterious figure, which they assumed was a patient. They began to catch up, growing closer and closer and closer.

Dequation began to grow more and more worried as they approached him. When, all of a sudden, they pulled him to the floor. He felt the shock echo around his body. What was going on? He, at that momment, felt something almost posses him. As if it were not Daniel and Louise dragging him to the ground, but a different, unearthly being.

As Dequation fell to the floor, Daniel and Louise stood tall over him, celebrating their sucsess. They began to tie him up with some nearby rope, purely for ease to carry him. They began to dag him away to the canteen.

Dequation kicked and screamed as he was dragged further and further away from his dream. His dream of becoming rich and famous. The bang of the canteen doors swung open and Dequation cried in agony. What was going on?

Chapter 17

Suspicions

Lisa wandered through the long lasting corridor that was a road to Clara's ward. Lisa followed the steps that the doctor took to get to her intended location. She started to get a turning feeling in her stomach. A feeling brewing up in her stomach, a nervous feeling as if she has never been here before, even though she visits every week. She kept following the doctor, following every turn and every door the doctor went through. Lisa start to recognise the route she was taking through the hospital, she knew that the next turning would be a left through the wooden door. This was something she didn't want to remember, she wanted her sister out of there.

Once she finally got to the ward after a long journey through the hospital, she stood waiting out side of the ward Clara was staying in. The doctor began to walk away until Lisa reaches to put her hand out and softly went to grab the doctors shoulder.

"I forgot to ask, how is Clara doing recently?" she asked. "She's been doing fine, she's also started speaking to more people on her ward recently. I think she's really improving." Lisa's smile grew across her face, she had never been so happy to find out things about her sister. She had hope within her that Clara would make it out soon.

Lisa pushed open the wooden door that was

separating the ward from the corridor, she stepped into the ward and all heads turned to her. The patients hoped that maybe the person walking through the door was someone to come and keep them company and ask how they are doing, they hoped that maybe it was someone to come and tell them that they are allowed out of the prison that they have been trapped in for months or even years for some of the people stuck in the ward. They wished they weren't there. Every eye that lay in the patients emotionless faces. followed Lisa across the room with every step she took. They saw her as an outsider, they questioned why she was still visiting her sister after putting her through her worst nightmare. How a person could be so caring to a soul that was so insane. Lisa knew everyone in the ward was looking at her, so she walked with her head facing down to the floor. She wondered what the people thought of her, she thought they would judge her for still checking up on Clara. No matter how many times she walked through the door she would never look the faces of the people who's mind worked just the same as Clara.

When Lisa got to Clara's bed, she felt a wave of relief. Even though Clara was just the same as all the other people laying in the ward. She felt a sense of her mum and dad when she was with Clara. She felt like there presences were still watching over Clara to see if the voice in her head is being silenced. Lisa believes it was the voice in Clara's head that did that to her parents and she believes that Clara will silence the voice in her head one day. Lisa sat on the chair that was paces beside Clara's bed. She placed her black leather mini backpack beside the weak legs of the wooden chair. "So, how has everything been this week?" Lisa asked while turning the chair towards Clara. The silence took over the room, Clara didn't reply. "Are you okay?" she asked again. Lisa's concerns started to rise.

Lisa looked up at Clara, she instantly knew something was not right, Clara had an intimidating grin that was growing across her face. Lisa

108

grabbed Clara's shoulder and started shoving Clara
to try and get her to stop her pulling the expression which was locked on her face. Clara wouldn't
look Lisa in the eyes. She didn't know what to
do, she wasn't being her normal self, she didn't
know if this was normal, she didn't know if she
should call the doctor. Lisa didn't know what
to do. Anxiety started to take control of her
body starting in her stomach, then rushing into
her heart. Quickly spreading across her arms and
hands making her palms sweat, then dropping
down to her legs which started to tremble and
trip.

Lisa jumped out of her seat and walked up
to the doctor, Lisa's head turned to Clara while
walking to the doctor to make sure she wouldn't
do anything while she wasn't looking at her. She
walked up to the doctor with unease. "Clara isn't
acting her normal self, I'm not sure what to do."
she explained. The doctor followed Lisa back to
Clara's bed wondering what could be wrong. The
doctor calmed down Lisa and began to explain

that it was nothing to worry about. "Its been happening quite often and its pretty normal as other patients have been doing the same." the doctor said. All the anxiety that was controlling Lisa's body flooded out.

Even though the doctor has reassured Lisa whatever was happening to Clara was normal, Lisa still had worries that it wasn't right for her to be doing it. She tried not to worry about it and remember what the doctor said that it was normal and not to worry about it.

Lisa sat there for the rest of her visit with Lisa, her right leg crossed over her left leg that lay on the chair. Her nails were slowly being chipped away as she sat picking at them as a way to take her mind off what Clara was doing.

Lisa said her goodbyes to Clara, picks up her backpack and waved to her as she walked back into the corridor. Lisa reached for her phone out of her bag and went to search up what happened to Clara to see if it was actually normal like the doctor stated. She searched it up and no results showed up. The anxiety that flooded out of her started to refill inside of her. She knew something wasn't right with her and started to worry about the other patients that it had been happening to as well. She didn't know if was going to stop or if it would happen for long periods each time. She wanted to know why it was happening and if it only happens to certain people.

Instead of going home straight away, Lisa sat in the waiting room so she could ask someone about it. Ask if anyone knows anything about it. She needed answers to what was happening. Her shoes started tapping on the floor patiently waiting for someone to walk in.

Chapter 18

The Preparation

Candles were lit, melting away the wax as the six pointed star was drawn on the floor, the pre-ritual chant was about so start. The smell of burning candles flooded the air, anticipation made the room fall silent. The canteen was not a work of art, only an eerie atmosphere of unwanted memories. As the candle started to burn down with little time left, Brooke took her chance to try and change things for the best, for the benefit of all of her friends. Brooke remembered why she was here in the first place, not because of any illness, but because people were manipulating her into thinking that she was in the wrong. She felt like a prisoner, trapped and scared. She didn't want another man to manipulate her in the way that others did, so this was her time to break the barrier, to prove to herself that after years of being controlled, she was finally in charge.

Brooke watched with fear as the ritual was set up, ready to take place. Elijah had no doubt in his mind of stopping the ritual so Brooke had to stop this now. The clock on the wall was a constant reminder of how trapped Elijah made her feel. Trapped inside of her own body. She felt sick at the thought of what could happen. After being referred to St Dymphna's years ago, Brooke had always taken things with a pinch of salt, knowing that everything that people believed about her would be a lie.

Brooke had always been a respected young girl who knew almost everyone in her town. Whatever she was doing, she had a joyful spring in her step and always treated others with respect. Every Saturday morning, she would walk through her little cobbled town and treat her neighbours to a pastry from the small corner shop bakery. She had lived with her heinous husband for years until she realised that something wasn't right. On several occasions, her husband made her believe that she was in the wrong, when actually he was the only one to blame. It got to the extent when he purposefully broke into their family home to turn the place upside down, only to prove that Brooke was mentally unstable and needed psychiatric support. Years went by and many court cases had taken place when finally the decision came to refer Brooke to St Dymphna's. Little did they know that he had paid a random witness to lie for him. All that her husband wanted was power over her, and all of this was happening over again in the blink of an eye.

Elijah had nearly finished preparing the ritual. The room made her feel claustrophobic as if she couldn't escape, her whole life was standing in front of her. Brooke was unaware of where her fate would take her next, but she knew that it wasn't going to be anywhere or anything good. Her shaken body felt like shattered ice as she clenched her fists against her body. Memories of her previous life were attacking her thoughts, she couldn't let Elijah get away with this. She thought of all of the good memories that had entered her life, although she struggled to think straight in the environment she was surrounded in. All that she wanted was to get out of this terrifying hospital and to travel the world. All that could cross Brooke's mind was the Santorini guide book she found in the library. Her chilled body fell to the ground as her muscles became paralysed.

It was getting too late! As Brooke was sitting up against the wall, sounds of anger flooded her head. These memories were too close to home for

Brooke, she felt traumatised. She curled up into a compact ball of fear, wanting all of this just to be one of her many nightmares she had experienced in hospital. She closed her eyes cautiously and counted to ten, still hearing the chanting of Elijah starting the ritual.

The chanting soon became unclear, with Elijah confidently chanting in fluent Egyptian. The chant rolled of his tongue, as if he had rehearsed it thousands of times before. Confidence surrounded his body as he continued with the chant. This couldn't be true, how could this even be happening? Had he been cursed already?

As the pre-ritual chant was coming to an end, Elijah harshly demanded Brooke to gather all of the patients together ready for the ritual. As much as Brooke hated the thought of doing this, she thought it might be a good idea to get them all together, so she knew exactly what was happening. All of this felt morally incorrect, but surely this was her only option. As she hesitantly walked around the dim hospital corridors, the patients

117

sat silently in their own narrow rooms, just staring into space. As much as Brooke wanted them all together, it wasn't an easy task. She transferred each unstable patient one by one into the canteen, some screeching and shouting with pain and anguish, others staring blankly into space.

After at least an hour, Brooke had finally gathered all of the patients together, who were now sat in a large circle around the six pointed hand drawn star. Silence flooded the room, sadness and grief filled the unresponsive bodies that were slumped into their navy blue plastic chairs. As though they had been hypnotised, they all aggressively stared into the centre of the circle, as if they knew their fate. Brooke's body was drowned in fearful sweat as she watched the patients suffer. She worriedly talked to the patients to try and get them to speak, but it quickly came to Brooke's attention that she would be virtually invisible to them As she didn't have an illness, she couldn't communicate very well with the others.

The canteen was brimming with sadness as the

walls felt like they were caving in with desperation for help.

The ritual was about to start, there was no way of escaping now. The sturdy silver doors were securely locked so no one else could enter. St Dymphna's was a very secure building, as you entered the intimidating reception area, you had to hand in your phone before you stepped through the main doors, with the exception of the doctors. Everything was controlled by a key card and face identification which was hard to fake in a place as protected as this. Brooke rubbed her head in desperation trying to figure out how to get hold of a key card. The room was layered in an unbearable heated mist, all of which was coming from the patients unreactive bodies. Brooke immediately needed to get hold of a key card, but the only person in this horrendous room who owned one was Elijah.

The patients were sitting as still as an unopened door whilst Brooke was scanning Elijah for the keycard. Elijah's appearance was a simple as a lavender suit and a paper white shirt. Brooke's eyes circled around his slumped body like a carousel, unable to stop mentally searching for the card. Her eyes promptly stopped as she located the card in his right jacket pocket, alongside his mobile phone. She sat in silence questioning herself on how to get the card. Brooke casually but carefully walked over to Elijah, swerving around the almost broken tables and chairs. She took a leap of faith over all of the isolated and abandoned objects and headed towards him. All that she needed to do now was to get the key card, but was her plan too good to be true?

Chapter 19

The Search

Lisa started to look around the black room with white blank walls and black leather seats lined up along the room. The silence was the only thing that filled the room. Lisa saw Nancy and George sat together across the empty room, she had no idea who these people were and had no idea these people would have know the answer to this mystery she was concerned about. She walked up to them and asked if anything weird was happening in the ward. Nancy and George looked at each other as fear plastered on their face, they looked back at Lisa wondering if she knew anything about what they were about to tell her and if she knew anyone who had been taken over by the book.

They finally told her what was happening after deciding she was probably one of the last people who could help them with their mystery. They began to explain what was happening. They told her that there was a magic book, it was thousands of years old, probably millions. No one knew anything about the book, all they knew was that it was from ancient Egypt which was affecting insane people and it was taking over the people of the hospital. Lisas heart had sunk within the unexplainable feeling taking over her body. She knew something was happening to Clara. She remembered what the doctor had said earlier: "Its been happening quite often and its pretty normal as other patients have been doing the same." Lisa knew Clara wasn't the only one being taken over by the book. They all come to the realisation that they needed to find the patients before it was too late and they need to find them soon.

Hysterically running through the waiting room following each other in a group, they pushed straight through the door that stood infront of them as if wasnt there, the doors slammed against the wall as they ran down the corridors. Every door they came upon they would slam their hands against it and shout "Let us in!" at the top of their lungs to see if they could get a response or hear anything that was happening in the rooms. All the doctors that were in the rooms further had no concerns about the loud bangs, they didn't even question it. They were so used to the patients being loud that they didn't answer when they banged on their doors.

Their feet dragged along the white marbled tiles that trailed along their journey to find the missing patients with them, their shoes squeaked with every leap they did down the corridor of horror. They kept banging at every door they came across. Over and over again... it was like a never ending tunnel of emptiness, it was like they were running away from nothing, like they were banging on the same door and expected a different response.

After traveling around the hospital for what felt like hours, they wiped the sweat that was made up of exhaustion and agitaton off their foreheads. They finally reached the canteen. Something was off, there was a vivid glow that was shooting under the door. The strong glow that was coming from the room behind the door projected onto their faces and an orange glare reflected into their eyes. A sound started to come from under the door, it wasn't a pleasant sound, it pierced their ears with every tune that they heard.

They realised the patients were in this room that was releasing the piercing noise and the unnoticeable light. They stopped banging for a second or so. They weren't too sure how to get to the patients from out of the trap but they knew that had to get in there before anything else weird started to happen. The feeling of distress and startle started to take over their bodys. Throbbing from banging on the countless doors, their hands dragged along their body as they started to turn a raw red. Their knees started to tremble and wear out out of fatigue.

Once again they started banging on the doors, except they got the response they had been looking for. It was an unrecognisable voice, as if it was someone who had just been summoned by some type devil. "Get away from the door!" announced a concealed identity. Instantly stopping as soon as the voice was heard, they stepped back from the door. They found themselves another mystery they needed to find the answer to.

They stuck to the plan and continued to bang on the door, they thought it would distract whatever this person or thing was planning on doing to the patients. They knew it wasn't the safest thing to do but they knew the thing they had to do was get into the canteen quickly.

Continuously banging on the door, their hands stung and inflamed but they couldn't stop. They realised the more they banged the more irritated the Demon would get. "Your body could be useful for this ritual!" he commented. They stopped in the blink of an eye. They knew what they were planning. It had to stop.

Chapter 20

Deadly Deviants

Nothing could be changed now, the ritual was about to start. As the pages nonchalantly turned in the book, lifeless things started to come alive. Chairs were lifted effortlessly from the ground and plates floated around the room like flying saucers. The room instantly became a whirlwind, the patients were the only things still steadily on the ground. The book itself was participating in this moment of madness. Simultaneously, another page turned, Brooke was unaware of what was going to happen next. She tried to communicate with the patients hoping that they would know what was going on, but nothing seemed to be working or helping matters at all. Sparks began to fly from the ancient ritual equipment that was placed in the middle of the canteen; they danced through the air towards the inhabitants of the hospital, backing them up into the walls. The sparks were the only form of light in the dinginess of the room. An eerie mist had began to surround them, floating overhead, it made the air thick and their throats seemed to be closing up as they stood there possessed.

Suddenly, one of the pieces of ancient ritual equipment that was standing in the middle of the room began to glow. A bright, fluorescent light was cast from it, lighting up the depressing gloom. Every time a page of the book turned over, the light flickered and buzzed slightly, which everyone in the room would have found highly concerning if they weren't being possessed. The light got stronger after every flicker of it, until it was almost blinding. Brooke covered her eyes and turned to face the wall, she was becoming increasingly worried by the second, she didn't know what to do. After about 5 minutes of standing with her back to thew ritual, Brooke heard a loud bang. She decided that she had to turn around to see what was going on. The piece of the ritual equipment that the light had been coming from had disappeared, along with the light that it had once held, however, the new sight that her eyes were met with was not a pleasant one.

Everyone was standing in a perfect circle, each persons movements mirroring the nexts, everybody's facial expressions matched perfectly. They were different people with the exact same actions, it was like they were completing a dance routine that they had been practicing for years until they were perfectly in-time with every movement that

129

they performed. Brooke jumped backwards startled as, without warning, everyone started chanting, and not in English. Brooke decided that they must be chanting some Egyptian curse or ritual, and she was sure that the more they chanted, the crazier the atmosphere became with plates spinning out of control in every direction and the mist seemed to be copying the movements of the robots. The robots, Brooke shivered at the thought, it described how they were acting but Brooke knew them all and knew that this was a serious problem that needed to be solved quickly. She looked to her left and saw five fellow patients and three doctors but she also saw that it would only take one second for disaster to stike.

As this horrifying thought crossed her mind, she realised that there were more things to worry about, if things didn't calm down a bit soon, the whole of the canteen might end up collapsing on them. Right as she thought this a stray plate whizzed past her, narrowly avoiding her head. It continued to spin out of control right towards the window. Brooke wanted to stop what as happening however, before she could even begin to think about how to do so, she heard a loud smashing sound before seeing sharp shards of glass flying in every direction. It was a miracle, she thought, that nobody had been badly hurt, well yet anyway. As plates and chairs swirled in loops overhead, Brooke's head was spinning with one thought; what was she going to do?

Brooke looked, startled, over her shoulder when she heard a muffled scream from the corner. Apparently so did everyone else as the chanting stopped and Brooke heard footsteps approaching her quickly. She realised that they were all heading over to were the scream came from, to Dequation. He was lying down in the corner of the canteen, struggling, tied up, screaming through his gag. There were spots of dried blood adorning all of his clothes. Brooke felt that he had probably been there for a while and she wondered how she hadn't noticed him there before. Brooke realised that Elijah was swiftly making his way over to where Dequation was lying defenceless, closely followed by Jamie, who, dragged Dequation across the floor and left him in a heap on the floor.

As soon as Jamie had walked away from Dequation, Clara began to place candles around his body and when she had them surrounding him, she began to light them. Fear blazed in Dequations eyes as he realised the trouble that he had just got himself into. He realised he was trapped. Lying tied up on the floor with the deadly flames of the candles threatening to lick his clothes. Dequation had not noticed, however, the body of Elijah standing over him, preparing to perform the ritual and he did not notice until the chants arose once more, as robotic and as creepy as ever. The sound of all the harmonised voices echoing off of the walls, Brooke covered her ears feeling like she was going to go crazy if she listened to it anymore.

As the chant went on it seemed to get louder and the louder the chant became, the higher the flames rose. Chairs whirled overhead, being flung in every direction by the raging mist. The sparks spat threateningly, backing people up in to the walls. As the flames of the candle grew higher, pools of wax began to form at the bottom of them, spreading stealthily towards the stiff and terrified body of Dequation, threatening to burn him. None of the patients or doctors showed any remorse or guilt at what they were doing, it was a very unsettling site, however, Brooke knew that if she managed to help them, and return them to their normal emotional state, they would be showing these emotions that they were currently lacking.

Brooke uncovered her ears when she felt that she heard a scream, to check if it was real or whether she was hallucinating. Her ears were not deceiving her although by the screams coming from Dequation, she may have wished that she was. If she didn't know that he had stolen the key card and probably got himself into this mess, she would have definitely taken pity on him. Elijah was drawing steadily closer to him, getting

ready to start the ritual. The other patients and
doctors chanted on, continuing their deadly tune.
Elijah drew closer still, towering over Dequation
like a human over an ant. Dequation's screams
continued, still muffled by his gag. Suddenly Elijah started to chant, it was different to the other
chant however it was just as eerie and robotic. After around one minute of Elijah chanting, Dequation's body slumped flat to the floor, seemingly
unconscious.

Suddenly, Brooke heard a knocking sound, it
was barely audible over the loud chanting that
was a occurring so she couldn't at first decipher
where it was coming from. She looked around desperately, feeling that she might be going insane.
Then, however, she spotted Brooke, Nancy and
George, knocking at the window of the waiting
room. She was fearful that if she let them in, they
would become just as possessed as the others however, she knew that they were probably her best
bet, she wouldn't be able to do it on her own, she
didn't know what to do. So Brooke slowly began

to make her way around the room, trying to keep to the shadows, she didn't want the others to find out what she was doing and try to stop her. A flying chair spun past her head, so close she could hear it whistle. Brooke realised that if George, Nancy and Lisa didn't have a solution, they were in deep trouble...

Chapter 21

Walking Into a Nightmare

After banging for what felt like hours, their knuckles were red raw from non stop hitting the walls and doors. "How long are we going keep banging for?" Lisa said very agitated.

"Not much longer, I don't think anyone is going to hear us, "Nancy said. Just as they were about to stop they heard footsteps coming close to the door, they saw the door handle which started fidgeting and shaking. With a bit of force the door opened and the very warm and musty air would hit you in the face because it was filled with smoke. Then as the door flew open, on the other side they saw Brooke. She was trembling with fear, her eyes were teary and she looked so exhausted from everything.

"Finally, " Nancy said quietly because she was overworked. Brooke stopped them all and told them about everything that was going on in the canteen and how it wouldn't be easy to get there but that they had to go back. They were unsure on leaving the waiting room because they didn't really know what to expect when walking to the ritual. After a small discussion they all decided that they needed to go to the canteen now. Since Brooke had left the canteen earlier, she dreaded to go back to see what was going on. As they left the waiting room area they started to hear the noises getting louder and louder from the ritual, this was putting more panic on their minds and was making their stomachs turn. The walls started shaking when the wind became stronger and started howling louder. The group quickly realised that getting in there was more difficult than they thought.

They were only one corridor away until they reached the canteen, chairs and tables were everywhere with furniture covering the floor, it was just all round messy and that made it a challenge to get to the canteen doors. "Watch where you're walking, it's not very safe here, " Brooke said with concern in her voice. The crunches underneath their feet from the broken glass and furniture was echoing throughout the corridor, bouncing on and off the walls. As they walked down the longest corridor in the hospital the noises started getting louder and louder. The glass on the floor was shining like a diamond when the sunlight hit it. After finally getting to the canteen doors safely they could see the destruction that has been caused in the canteen. Broken pieces of plastic and wood were all over the hallway, messy just like a bomb had gone off. The glass was shattered over the floor like pieces of ice cubes which wouldn't melt. The smell of smoke filled the air from the flames of the ritual, it was pungent and would just get stronger and stronger as they moved closer to the canteen doors. The air became thick and musty making it difficult to breathe. Their fear started to rise as they reach the canteen doors, they were in suspense which was causing their stomachs to turn.

Brooke tried to push open the doors but soon found out it wasn't going to be that easy for them to get in . She managed to get Elijah's card earlier but she didn't realise that to get in with the key card, you also needed a fingerprint to open the door. Everyone tried to push open the two doors but nothing would move them. "The doors won't open, I don't know how we are supposed to open them because something is jamming the

doors closed." Brooke said annoyed. "HELP!"
"HELP!" they were shouting over and over again
but there was no sign that anyone was coming to
help them. All that you could hear was banging and crashing and the occasional plate flying
through the window. "CRASH!' is all they could
hear as another plate or piece of furniture hit the
wall. Each bang would make everyone tremble
in fear because they didn't know what to expect
next. As they looked through the broken glass
windows they could see the sparks, flames and different colours going everywhere off the set up of
the ritual. They couldn't believe their eyes when
they saw the mess the hospital was now in.

After trying everything that they could to get
someone's attention the group decided to try and
force the door down with something. Brooke picked
up a leg of a chair and started to try and break
the door down but it wasn't working. The chips
of wood from the chair leg was flying all over the
room. The atmosphere of the room was very tense
and tight. The loud bangs and crashes were filling

the room. Glass crunching every step that they took. Their hands were inflamed and swollen but they couldn't give up. Pure panic and fear was on all their faces, worried about what was going to happen next. Brooke started to panic as they got closer and closer to opening the door because of what was happening in the canteen before she left. Finally, after all of the banging and crashing, the doors flew open and they were greeted by the ritual. The sparks were almost blinding and the atmosphere was very eerie and skin crawling. All of their faces dropped when they realised what they are walking into. They were walking into their next nightmare and there was no turning back.

Chapter 22

The Counter Curse

Suddenly, the door burst open and George and Nancy sprinted into the room followed by Lisa and Brooke. A look of pure panic crossed their faces as they realised that they had just walked into a nightmare.

Sparks flew from a strange setup of what seemed to be ancient ritual equipment, from the middle of which Dequation's body could be seen, tied up and motionless, lighting up the gloomy canteen. Thin whisps of mist swirled eerily around like silent ghosts floating through the night. Lisa slowly backed into a corner, a look of pure terror upon her ashen face. A tear slid slowly down her cheek as she looked into the glassy eyes of her possessed sister's mad face.

Nancy reached into her pocket and pulled out a crinkled piece of paper that looked to have been pulled out of an old book. It was written in hieroglyphs and although Nancy could have translated it, she couldn't actually speak it. However, Nancy knew someone who could. Her soft grey eyes scanned the room before falling upon Leo. She walked swiftly over to him and began to speak gently to him in a soft voice.

"You need to read this, " she explained kindly but leaving no doubt that she meant what she was saying.

Leo stared blankly into her eyes, no emotion crossing his face. "You need to read this, " repeated Nancy a little louder this time, half pleading with him, half trying to convince him that he has to do it, a firm look settling on her welcomimg face. Leo looked scared now as he looked around and his hand started shaking slightly. His whole body began to twitch and he began to vigorously shake his head from side to side. The idea of it seemed to be making him deranged. Nancy was visibly worried now, her eyes were full of alarm and anxiety.

George and Brooke hurried across the dull room to Nancy and Leo.

"Leo we know you can do it, you have to, " spoke Brooke quietly, in a small voice that had turned rather frail in her old age. Leo looked despairingly into all of their faces.

"Please Leo, you are the only one that can do this, you have to, you will be seen as a hero, surely you want that, " came George's voice trying

145

to turn the situation into a positive for Leo who looked apprehensively at George, however, there was a slightly braver look set on his face and he stopped shaking and twitching so much.

"Please, " was Nancy's final word to Leo. Slowly but surely, Leo's shaking of the head began to turn into a slight nod.

Nancy took Leo's hand and placed the crinkled piece of paper in it. Leo looked at her with a face full of annoyance and apprehension. Nancy, however, felt relief flow through her body like a river, a look of thankfulness glowing on her face. Leo, after one last glare at Nancy, began to grudgingly read the counter curse. It sounded like some ancient chant that people would use to summon demons thousands of years ago. George felt the hairs on the back of his neck stand up. He took a step back from Leo as Nancy and Brooke did the same. Leo's voice sounded robotic, as if he was on auto-pilot and George noticed that he was slowly getting louder and more confident in what he was doing.

After about thirty seconds of Leo reading, everything seemed to calm down. The amount of mist hanging over their heads lessened along with the amount of sparks flying from the ancient ritual equipment. It seemed to go on for hours, the chant, but nobody could be sure. It felt like torture to anybody listening, making your eardrums throb and feel like they were going to explode. Lisa had her hands over her ears, she looked to be going insane. After what seemed like forever, the chant seemed to be coming to an end, however, Leo stopped abruptly, a look of utter horror plastered to his face. He looked around panicking shooting furtive looks around the room. "Carry on!" urged Nancy. He did do so however, he looked terrified of something unknown to everyone else. As he finished the last to line of the chant Nancy gasped,

"s..somebody has t..to be s..sacrificed, " she stammered, the colour draining from her face.

The whole canteen erupted and the sound of it was deafening.

"Alexander can die, he murdered three people, he deserves it!" shouted Clara.

"What about you, you murdered your parents and were the first to try to give up somebody else's life!? You know that it should be you! That's why you're pinning the blame on somebody else! To protect yourself!" screamed Jamie.

"She didn't mean it, she hated the therapy, she never meant to hurt anyone, besides you are one to talk, you killed somebody just the other day!" yelled Lisa in her sisters defence.

"The only reason you are defending her right now is because she is your sister! Murder is an inexcusable crime! I know that I murdered somebody but I swear I was being possessed, I didn't mean too but we all know that Clara has anger issues, she blows up at the slightest comment that slightly upsets her, the world would be a better place without her in it!" retorted Jamie in a low hiss.

"Why has nobody mentioned my dad, I mean he is the reason that we are in this mess in the first place, "George mumbled grumpily to Nancy, who gently leaned against his arm to help comfort him.

"Don't worry, he will get what he deserves at some point, " promised Nancy.

"Jamie stop making things up! You did that because you are evil and you decided to take out the pain you were feeling about your dads death and the built up anger aimed at your mother on all of us here. You don't even make an effort to be friendly!" Clara spat bitterly at Jamie.

"Just because you talk to people to try and convince them that you are a good person doesn't mean that you are and just because I prefer to have time to myself doesn't mean that I'm evil!" replied Jamie.

"Don't you dare talk about my sister like that! She is a good person and right now I'm getting the impression that you are jealous of her, I mean why else would you keep making things up about her!?" Lisa responded, her face still colourless.

"Will everyone please stop throwing insults

around or we will never get anywhere!" stated Nancy, loud enough for everyone to hear but her voice had a previously unseen aggression so she immediately made the room fall quiet. Everyone began to look around feverishly in the deafening silence, everyone unsure and everyone on edge. Suddenly a small voice came out of the shadows, it was so quiet that surely nobody could have heard it but they did.

"I'll do it, " came the barely audible voice, "Sacrifice me..."

As the body to the voice stepped forwards, everyone gasped, but they couldn't be surprised, they should have guessed. As the pure definition of a selfless person stepped forwards, George and Nancy looked at each other grievously, the person so bravely standing infront of them did not deserve to die and they both knew it. However, they also both knew that there was no changing this persons mind, and they knew that nobody else would offer their own life, they knew that no matter how heavy it was weighing on their hearts, it was the only way forward. Looking around the room their wasn't a single person who didn't look sick to their stomach, silent tears rolling down their bloodless cheeks. "Don't worry about me, it's for the best, " came Brooke's innocent voice as she took one more step forwards, her expressions serene, even as she walked towards her end. For a few seconds, nothing happened, everything stayed as it was, but not for long. In the blink of an eye the unsettling mist swooped down and surrounded Brooke and before anyone knew what was happening, her body was flying, swirling in the mist, the fierce sparks spitting their poison at her. Louise screamed and Alexander jumped backwards, this was an image that was going to live unwanted in the back of all of their minds.

What was seconds seemed like hours, Brooke's heroic body floating overhead spinning in sickening circles. After what felt like eternity, Brooke's body dropped to the floor, and that was where it stayed, limp and lifeless. Nancy grasped George's hand, tears cascading down her cheeks. George's bright blue eyes had lost their shine and were staring solemnly at the heap on the floor; he gripped Nancy's hand tightly. He showed no emotion, but it was clear to see through the blank look on his face and see how much he was really hurting.

Chapter 23

Betrayal

The atmosphere in the canteen was depleted. The silence echoed off the walls. The lights slowly began to stop flickering and the cloud of smoke and sparks that once stood tall in then air like a ruler looking over his subjects cascaded to the ground. The remains of the ritual spoke volumes to the patients. Smashed tables, flickering candles, bloody ropes. Everything served as a reminder of the evil that had just overtaken them. Guilt flooded the room, even from people who were not involved. Jamie stared down at her feet, too ashamed and embarassed to look her former victims in the eye.

Slowly, the formerly overtaken people began to return to the body of their original selves. Groans, screams and shouting escaped from their seemingly lifeless bodies. Their previously dead faces began to run with a vivid glow instead of the past looks of emptiness and the robotic smiles. Their veins began to run with a drizzle blue tint and their eyes reclaimed their original chandelier like gleam. A flood of taffy pink tones rushed through their faces, planting the seeds of life and joy throughout their faces.

However, not all was pleasant, as Elijah still looked guilty. He had been, unlike the others, awoken up to nightmares of death, blood and trauma. He had realised the pain he put his son through, the added trauma he had given the people he swore to help. He felt like his entire good purpose had gone to waste. How much money had been spent on him? How many people had truly cared for him, only for him to abandon them. For him to give up on them. His family had left him, he had violently murdered the love of his life, the only person who stood up for him. When everyone had left him, Kate was there. What would she say right now? And George, the boy who just wanted a family, the boy who was innocent, Elijah had failed him. Elijah had failed everyone. He fell to his knees with sorrow.

"George, George, please, listen to me, I'm so sorry George, I had no idea I swear, I didn't mean it, " he cried out. George walked over to him, a stern expression on his face. Why does his dad only just realise what he's put him through? He could never understand. No one could understand.

"Dont beg for my forgiveness now, You have no idea what you put me through, " George responded coldly.

"But son..., " Elijah pleaded.

"Do not call me your son, we are nothing alike. Me and you are purely related by blood. Me and you have no emotional bond. You do not get to call me your son, " George replied heartlessly.

"Look, George, I tried. I really did. You don't understand how bad I feel right now. I didn't mean to murder your mother, it was all the book. Do you think I wanted to kill the only woman I've loved? Do you want to know the truth? I cried while holding that knife. I cried when I pushed her into the lake. I had zero control over my body. And about not being there for you, you know that I just have a demanding job. My life has never been that easy and you know that. Why are you acting like this? I guarantee you I miss Kate even more than you. Just take me back, accept me as your Dad. We can put it all behind us, I'll always be there for you. Just take me back, please son, " Elijah begged.

George stared at him with a look of pure shock.

How dare his 'Dad' say that to him? Like he has any idea what George is going through.

"What did you just say to me?!" George roared, "How dare you act like you even miss my mum at all! You are doing the same thing you always do. Pin the blame on me, yet again, because you know your guilty. You'd get the whole world killed if it weren't for me, you know that right? You, at forty three years old, still need your seventeen year old motherless son to come and babysit you. You're mentally incapable of taking care of yourself that you need me to come and do it for you, isn't that right? I can't even bare to look at you, " George screamed, all the emotion pouring out of his aching heart.

An echo of shock flooded the room. No one could begin to comprehend all the pain and suffering George had been put through by Elijah.

"You can't even look at me in the eyes, Dad, you can't even look at me because you know I'm right, how pathetic must you be, " George said in a mocking tone. Elijah continued to stare at the

157

ground. He was kneeling on the canteen floor, like an abandoned king. He could have had it all. He knew that deep down it was his fault, he'd been too power hungry in life that he was too naive to notice he had it all in the first place. Maybe, in a different universe, they would have got along. George didn't truly hate his dad after all, it was impossible too, but in this very moment that was all he could feel. In a way it felt good, the man who had caused all his hurt was kneeling before him. But George noticed his face, that smug smile he had on him, and suddenly it clicked. Elijah wasn't really sorry. He just had no one.

This made George feel an emotion that he simply couldn't put into words. It was pure hate, pure disgust, pure anger. He couldn't even look at Elijah without getting a rush of it. It was the complete opposite of love. An emotion so strong that everyone in the room could feel it. George knew what he had to do in that moment. It was the only way he could cure his many years of pain that had been inflicted on him. In a flood of rage,

George kicked Elijah square in the face.

George felt no emotion about the kick. Infact, it felt rather good. So he decided to do it again. And again. And again. And again, until he felt he had no more kicks left in him. By now, Elijah, who George no longer saw as his dad, but rather as the man guilty of his pain, was unconscious. It felt, in a weird way, satisfying, to George that he was like this. So good infact that George dug deep inside himself and picked up a shard of a broken canteen window from the floor. The shard just fit so perfectly into his hand, it gave him a strange feeling, as if the shard was a mere extension of his arm, a vessel he could use to exert his raw emotions onto the man that had caused them in the first place. George, without a shred of mercy, brought the shard up past his head, and struck Elijah's heart perfectly, leaving an oddly shaped wound through Elijah's chest.

No words escaped Elijah's mouth when he died. He did not have a clear last breath, or inspirational last words. All that remained was an empty shell of a body, which perfectly mirrored Elijah's alive self. An empty shell of a man, who disregarded his son. The canteen went quiet at the time of his death. George, a seventeen year old boy, who had just made himself become an orphan, didn't look upset. Nancy ran up and hugged him, she wanted to be there for him at all costs, but George showed no emotion still. He hugged Nancy back, and rested his hand on the back of her head, pulling her closer to him. But he did not do it for his comfort. He did it because he couldn't bare the thought to have himself turn out like Elijah. In that moment, all he cared about was hoping that there would never be another Elijah Carter.

Chapter 24

Deja-Vu

The restless crowd for the annual fishermen's market in Aswan pushed through the river-side port. The crowd was always like this at this time of year, after all, this market was one of the busiest in the entire country of Egypt. The atmosphere was ecstatic, hundreds of people pushing

161

through the poorly made barriers despite the hardened efforts of the Egyptian National Police to contain it. Many new boats were still coming in as well, all carrying the same cargo: tonnes and tonnes of Nile perch, the chosen breed of fish for the citizens of Aswan.

"Pull! Pull! Pull!" a fisherman screamed, "The crowds are waiting and you aren't helping! Every fisherman needs to be putting his stock in them markets immediately!"

Zuri sighed.

"Always the men, always the men, " she complained.

"Shut up Zuri, " her Dad replied, "You're always complaining, you need to know that it's just the way life is here. Be lucky that you aren't expected to do the amount of work a man has to do."

Zuri exhaled, she knew she couldn't let her dad treat her like this, but she had no other choice. Besides, she didn't need anymore stress on the day of the market.

"Look Zuri, I know it annoys you, but one day you'll grow up and learn that life just works better this way, okay?" her Dad said peacefully, he knew that Zuri didn't like being treated like a young girl, but that's what she was at the end of the day. His words would make her annoyed, but they both knew that Zuri didn't have enough power to fight back, and would only end up hurting herself. As the boat neared the port, Zuri left to go and gather customers, while her Dad stayed to offload their cargo. If sales go smoothly here, they might be able to afford something other than fish and rye bread.

Zuri found an area in the heart of the market to position herself, that way she could attract maximum customers to her stall. As the police finally collapsed the barrier, floods upon floods of people hurriedly rushed towards her position.

"Come get your fish! Come get your fish!" Zuri shouted, "Only the finest Nile Perch available here! Freshly caught from the pure Egyptian Nile!"

Zuri didn't seem to be attracting many customers to her and her father's stall, but it didn't upset her too much, she knew that this was how it goes. Every. Single. Year. But this year, something felt different. She felt a constant ringing in her ears. A constant sound that she just couldn't seem to shake off. She had tried the usual tactics to calm the noises. After all, she had had this situation happen to her many times, with her psychosis. But it felt somewhat different this time. A noise she couldn't put down to her mental disorders, or the ambient noise of the shouting market crowd beneath, but rather the voice from a different creature.

The voice started off quiet, as if it didn't want to hurt her, as if it instead wanted to protect and nurture her. But after a while, the voice grew to an unspeakably loud volume, as if someone were shouting directly into her ear drum. The pain was immense, she felt as if her brain would explode through her ears at any second, like a time bomb about to go off. Desperately, she fell to her knees, not knowing how to cope with the agony that was reflecting throughout her brain.

Suddenly, the voice whispered a cure. A way to stop the pain, intact, a way to cure all her pain. "Listen Zuri...we can help you...go to the great statue of Ramesses...trust us now, " the voice said. Zuri couldn't refuse this offer. She followed the orders unknowingly. In a way, she had zero control over her body. Her limbs did not ache as she walked. She could not feel her hand as it opened up one of the gates connecting the market to that main roads of Aswan. She let the voices carry her corpse, she let them overtake her, under the idea that it was only temporary. She could regain control easily, or so she thought.

Once she reached the statue, she saw a book, half buried in the glowing sand, while the sun reflected its saffron tones onto the worn leather of the book.

"Pick it up, " whispered the voices, "Learn about my story, I am the great pharaoh Ramesses II." Eagerly, she read the book, the voices translated the ancient hieroglyphs into words, and sent every word travelling through her body, flowing through her veins, into her heart, accepted into her soul. She felt like the book had become a part of her, it gave her a feeling of power, a feeling of strength and leadership. As if she had become omnipotent and had no one who could challenge that.

"Now you've heard my story, Join us. We can rule over this world together." the voice offered. Zuri didn't even have to think twice about the offer, she accepted blindly. She picked up the book for the second time, and began to read it again. This time, truly taking in the words. The photos. The spells.

She sat reading the book for what seemed like eternity. As if she had never not known about the book's existence, it felt like an extra part of her, an extension of her hand, her brain perfectly mapped onto the yellowing pages. She was entranced by it, without a doubt, it completed her. It completed her so much she had to take it home, so she put it in her bag and went to travel back to the markets. However, she started to feel light-headed as something came upon her, like she had a second consciousness, or like she was being ma-nipulated by a foreign presence. Almost as if it was a strong feeling of deja-vu. What could go wrong?

Printed in Great Britain
by Amazon

80682835R10099